BABAR
THE MAGICIAN

LAURENT DE BRUNHOFF

Harry N. Abrams, Inc., Publishers

Babar, the king of the elephants, has been taking magic lessons.

Now he is ready to put on a magic show for the children. Pom, Flora, and Alexander invite all their friends to the palace to see the show.

First Babar puts his
top hat on a table.

When he picks it up, two doves fly out!

Then Babar asks for a helper.
Flora steps onto the stage and
Babar hides her under his cape.

When Babar lifts the cape—
surprise! Arthur is standing
in Flora's place!

Then Babar asks, "Who will help me with my next trick?"

"I will!" cries Zephir the monkey.

Babar waves his magic wand. He softly says, "Slee-ee-ee-eep . . ." and Zephir falls asleep.

Then Babar waves his wand again. Zephir, still asleep, begins to float off the ground!

But what is this? Zephir is flying out of the room! Babar is so surprised he doesn't know what to say.

Zephir floats across the street.

He flies through an open window . . .

...and floats across a room. Cornelius and the Old Lady are playing chess—they didn't expect any visitors!

Zephir flies out through a back window.

Then he flies over a country field
and breaks through an artist's canvas!

Zephir still doesn't wake up. He leaves the furious painter and flies across the river.

A fish bites his tail and escapes
from two hungry ducks.

Babar and Arthur finally catch up with Zephir and the fish.

Babar waves his magic wand and shouts, "WAKE UP, ZEPHIR!"

That does it! Zephir awakes in midair, falls down . . .

...and lands on Babar's head!
"Where am I?" he asks.

Everyone laughs. Zephir
doesn't remember a thing!

Design by Celina Carvalho

Production Manager: Jonathan Lopes

Library of Congress Cataloging-in-Publication Data

Brunhoff, Laurent de, 1925-
Babar the magician / Laurent de Brunhoff.
p. cm.
Summary: Babar takes magic lessons and puts on a show for his family and friends.
ISBN 0-8109-5863-5
[1. Magic tricks—Fiction. 2. Elephants—Fiction.] I. Title.

PZ7.B82843Babi 2005
[E]—dc22
2004012651

Printed and bound in China
10 9 8 7 6 5 4 3 2 1

Harry N. Abrams, Inc.
100 Fifth Avenue
New York, NY 10011
www.abramsbooks.com

Abrams is a subsidiary of
LA MARTINIÈRE
GROUPE